Ulrich Schaffer

with open eyes

Text and Photography by
Ulrich Schaffer

with open eyes

March 4, 1988

Dear Jenny,
Good wishes to you in your
new job!
Promise to keep in touch?
Love,
Claudia

HARPER & ROW, PUBLISHERS, SAN FRANCISCO
Cambridge, Hagerstown, New York, Philadelphia
London, Mexico City, São Paulo, Sydney

1817

Permission to photograph on
the Navajo reservation (cover
photo) courtesy of Navajo Film
& Media Administration,
Window Rock, Navajo
Nation, AZ.

FIRST EDITION

Cover and interior design
by Tony Agpoon Design,
San Francisco.

Library of Congress Cataloging in Publication Data

Schaffer, Ulrich.
    With open eyes.

    I. Title.
PR9199.3.S26W5 1982   811'.54   81-48213
ISBN 0-06-067073-8   AACR2
ISBN 0-06-067074-6 (pbk.)

82 83 84 85 86 10 9 8 7 6 5 4 3 2 1

Come,
be the one for me.
Let yourself be moved,
step into my life.
We will discover
where life renews itself,
and where death still blooms in us.

Don't be afraid,
yes be afraid,
I am too.
If we share our fear
it will turn to life.

I have chosen to see the world
with open eyes,
to experience impermanence,
to die in the constant change of images,
to come to life while resisting
the spread of impossibility,
that hovering friend

to see,
to be seen,
and to see more,
to penetrate that loose covering
obscuring truth,
to allow the eye to wander freely
and to watch it return to itself
and far beyond that narrowness
until seeing becomes effortless
in the merging of beholder and beheld

because all seeing is
being seen.

Let us put on the jewels of the sun,
decorate ourselves with light,
and in the light
the word will step forward in brilliance.
And in the word
the flesh will open up
as deliverance,
as life,
as light.

Today we want to believe
that the little dirt on our shoes
is nothing but a memory
of moments rushed past
and that behind them
we were always children
in the hands
of an unbelievably tender father

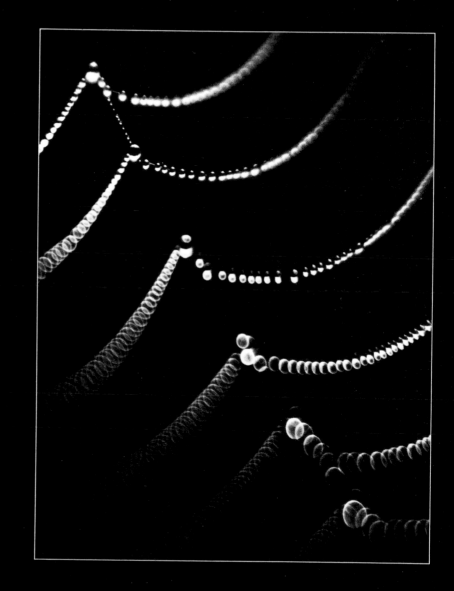

We are so vanishingly small
against the largeness of life
that our fear grows daily,
but our love also
has unthought of chances to bloom.

When life demands too much
we become strong and enter new territory,
and armed with rope and hooks
we take on the sheer cliff.

In life we lie as in a wound
stripped of all,
allies in the beautiful hard battle.
Brothers at last.

This is a landscape
which I discover in solitude.
To come to know myself
I must leave you behind.

Here I will search for my shadow
to overcome my fear of it.
Here I will see
if I have learned to die.
Here I will take the plunge
to know what Darkness is.
Here I will not call on the sun
but endure the secrets.

I see that you want to help me,
but that must not be.
This is one of the paths
I have to walk alone.

And yet I want you to know
that I subject myself to this
because you, your energy,
reach into the secrets.

Suddenly your energy is with me.
Because I am the wanderer
I am the foot in this landscape,
but you are the eye.

There are days
on which the world is empty.
Almost everything is air.
A few shadows render the landscape real.
Otherwise there is only the coming and going
of aimless thoughts.
I am caught between things,
not-here-anymore and yet-not-there.
The emptiness is unfillable.

You will reach me only with difficulty.
The telephone will ring in vain.
All messages will fall into that emptiness.
You call my name.

But do not give up.

I am on my way
to call and love into being
a new way of relating
among all things.

Over the nearby hills
the Old and New One is looking.
He has the form of the trees,
of the grasses,
your form, my friend,
the emptiness of the air.

He is the overflowing One.

On every path lies a secret
and in every decision
questions rise up
with fire and freedom.

On some paths I do not find you
and remain lonely,
a hand without eye,
an eye without foot.

The landscape is transformed
into a picture puzzle
in which I can't see you.
I am afraid of losing my way.
With pain and fear
I experience the silence
into which my path descends.

And yet,
because I can't find you,
because I can see only signs of you,
but not you,
because my thoughts
circle around your absence,
you are here

as cliff and meadow
as cloud and habitation.

From a sea of narrow waving stalks
no bread can be baked.

First there is the cutting—
   not only wound
   but giving up of life,
then the gathering—
   one stalk among thousands
   without specialness,
then the bundling—
   being bound against one's will,
   thrown and pierced with pitchforks,
placed in sheaves to dry—
   under the sun
   drying out all life,
then the threshing—
   beaten to separate kernel and chaff
and then, as if this were not enough,
each kernel is broken further
and only of the flour
   which reminds no one
   of the sea of waving stalks
bread is baked
and will nourish us.

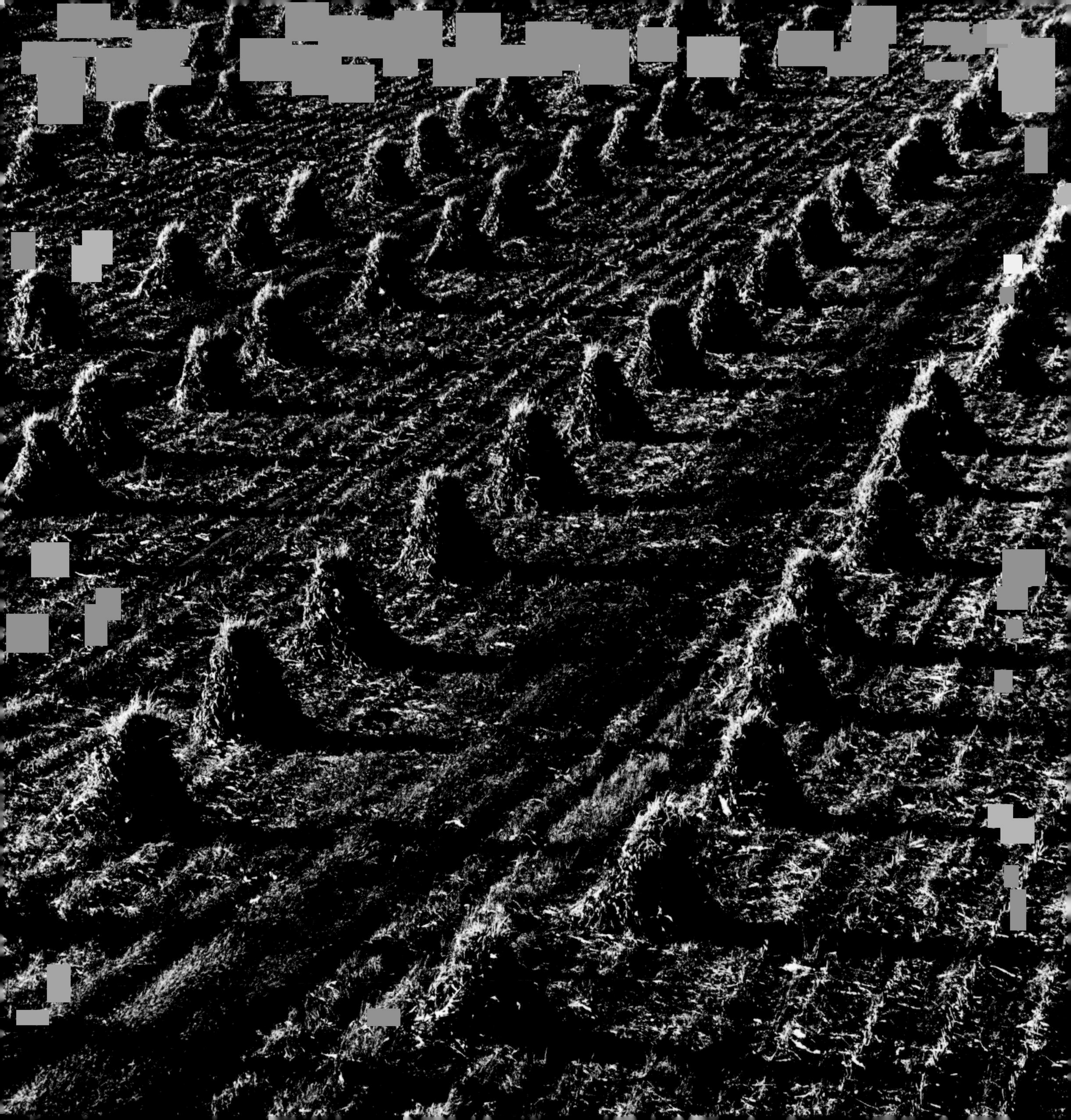

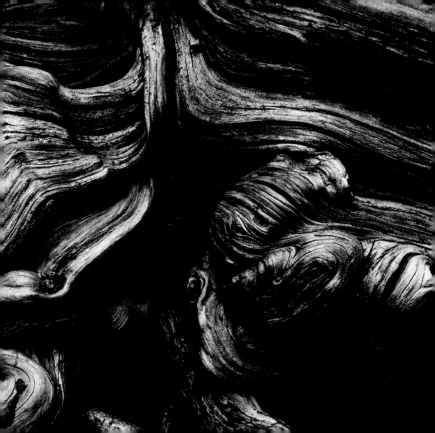

The knots and entanglements,
the restraints of life,
the search for ground water
striking only impervious rock,
the moaning and battling
at breaking point,

and all the while,
with irresistible force,
with definiteness as though predestined,
pushing up a trunk and branches,
blossoms and fruit
into the blue
and into the cracking thunder

(like nothing unusual)
in faith
and hope
a whole life long.

Even the stones
fall into the sky.
Nothing holds them back
from their upward tumble.
I also want to say
what everything in me is yearning for.
You are my witness and much more.

After all words
(the novels of our lives),
after all glances
(the open eyes of love),
after all sighs
(yours silent and mine loud),
after all the hardness
(the stony doors of the heart),
after the uncountable deaths
(the disappointments like knives),

there is only the stormy yearning
for him
who is life,
and nothing,
nothing,
will hold us back
from him.

Sometimes it seems to me
that the sky is filled with fists.
Threats arise menacingly
from everywhere.

The most secure begins to waver.
Clouds have a way of frightening.
Warnings stand like specters.
Darkness subjugates the world.

Then I wish that you would endure with me,
that words would remain familiar,
that I would still have a place
in your deep inner eyes.

Then I need, more than ever,
to discover the thread
that leads from him to you
and right through my fear
to a reconciliation of heaven and earth.

The world is enchanted.
Everything has become strange to me.
I have never been here.
I don't even recognize myself anymore.
I have an inkling but no more.

Be my mirror
(just look at me)
and tell me that you recognize me.
In your eyes I will recognize myself.
You call me forth
with your love.

I want to believe
that you can see wings growing on me,
I only feel the pain of breaking.
Give me courage, be more than mirror.
Let nothing in your eyes be broken,
the light must stand as solid as a rock,
so that the new can grow in me.

I shed what I have been,
and like a butterfly
that's left its form,
I now can fly.

Boldly we will conquer the world,
the world in us,
the one we have never walked on.

We will beckon uncounted dying
with a naked hand,
like a winterbird,
and live like the grain
that fell into the ground
and died
and lived.

The heart is wild
and wild the life
that tames it.

Against the sky
we are all silhouettes.
We are fingers stretched out,
words looking for listeners.
We are skin wanting to be touched.

And under our fears
we are screams
striking the sky
and then falling back on the screamers
like death by suffocation.

Do you recognize me
as your twin scream?
Will you help me
change my fear into wisdom?
Will you be the touch
that calls my skin to life?
Will you lure words
across my lips?
Will you be the heart
my fingertips encounter?
Will you be the color
compassionately encircling the world
like a large wave?

*Be patient with me
even when I am cold
and reject you.
Coldness has closed me
for fear of breaking yet again.
I do not want to freeze
and so do not expose myself.*

*If you want to open me
you must surround me with warmth.
Then I will open up, melt
and allow you to enter my world.*

*But you have to be serious
because if I turn cold again
my coldness with its fear
will freeze you.
We will both become stiff
in the abuse of words
and in feigned closeness.*

*A silent devastation
will engulf us
in which all motion will stop.*

Let me invite you to the place
where the light lies gently on all forms.

Let us stop time,
just be here,
let questions remain questions
and sense the density of life
from moment to moment,
shed the past and future like bothersome weights
and take hold of the present
    fine-fibered
    packed full of riches
    symphony of colors and forms
like heaven fallen to the earth.

We have nothing but this moment.
All loving and living
must happen now.

Holding on.
I am soft against the rock
and small against the ruthless weather.

There are days
on which I push roots down in vain.
Nothing holds. The rock is rejection.
Everything is wind.

Then it can be enough
to write your name,
or to hear your voice
caress my name,
to sense our hands in each other's.

Then I take courage
to sink my thoughts like teeth
into this landscape,
even when it rejects me.
I am undisturbed
that the weather is against me
and that the rock
will take a thousand years
to turn into soil
from which I can draw my nourishment.

And when you look at me
and we trust enough
to allow our gazes to sink into each other,
treasure in the depth of the ocean,
then I am not frightened by tomorrow.
The moment is holy
and bears enough joy and weight.

I will put down my roots in you
and together we will blossom.

Will you stand by me?
Will you throw yourself
into the search for more,
into the penetration of form and color,
into the lonely, resistant landscape?

If you do,
loneliness will become bread
for both of us.
Forms and colors
will surrender their secrets
and in our tumble into life
we will not be shattered.

You are more valuable to me
than you think.
You remind me of all that is yet to come.

Everywhere life pales
and steps back.
I can only surmise
where and how things will continue.
Unclarity settles on my world.
I have lost my way
in these inaccurate coordinates.
My energy
drains like water
from an overturned bottle.

That is why
I turn to you
in the hope
of being swept along by you
to risk the jump
back into life.

And if on other days
the world shuts you out
I will
be there
for you.

He leads us together,
lifts us out of the lostness
    in which we could not find each other,
gives us arms
    to let our beings
    flow toward each other,
gives us eyes
    to become lost in each other,
gives me a heart of flesh
    into which you can fall with your need,
gives me feet
    to find my way to you.

Come,
let us be moved
by the mover of all things.

I met you
in the vulnerability of your eyes,
in your dreams of redemption,
    visible around the corners of your mouth
and in your words,
    opened towards silence.

We opened ourselves wide,
became soft and gentle
like children bedded into the morning
and our heaviness turned into wings.

Now we dispense with the rules
of the solid ground,
plant somersaults in the air,
learn to fly between high wires
without a net,
held only by that precise timing
which is love.

Now we can rest in each other's eyes
and wait for love to relinquish
more images
which will transport us
to the heart of light,
to meet ourselves.

I have known
the overwhelming yearning
to be complete
and the temptation
to seek my completion in you,
to extract from you
what I am missing
in an act of abuse.

But today I feel strong enough
to delve into the deep recesses of myself,
to brave all fears,
to win time over to my side,
and to find my completion
in that hidden kingdom
established in me
before my time began.

And yet I have needed you
to learn that I must do without you
as my ultimate act of love for you
and me.

Can you see me
in the lostness of this landscape—
a small person,
much too afraid,
much too weak to hold my ground
against the devouring sea,
against the blinding sun
and against the teeth of my own thoughts.

I can already see myself as driftwood
    in the grinding waves,
and as a blind man
    in the unmerciful corona of the sun,
and as one driven and torn
    by my straying thoughts.

Can I call you to join me in the picture?
There is always room for you inside my fear.
If we are two, the landscape will not swallow us.
I am the muscle, you are the eye,
the waves will not grind us to sand.
You are my shadow, I am your compass,
the sun will not blind us.
With you I can complete all my thoughts,
and wolves that tear
turn into lambs that save.

We will populate this landscape
with splendor.
With large letters, we will write into the sand:
we are swimming,
we are living,
we are singing.

I have to protect my life on countless frontiers.
Worlds come rushing in,
choke me, flow over me,
and it is difficult not to be overpowered.

I am desert grass
in constant battle with the sand.
Each of my blades is a triumph,
each day like a year on my calendar.

And sometimes
when the grains of sand have me in their grip
I call for you.
The God who leads me to green pastures
seems to be so distant.
Only a hand of flesh and blood can help me.

And when I have survived everything
because you were eye
when I would have run into walls,
or hand
when I was too afraid to hold on,
then I know that God came, disguised in you.

Each experience has a frontier
from which I can see you and him better.

I twist myself
to give the wind
no place to attack,
the unmerciful weather
no exposure.

The shape I have assumed
is beautiful
beyond outer beauty,
visible only to the inner eye.

It will require your solid will
and unwavering stamina,
powered by distant illuminations,
to embrace such twistedness
for long.

Only the light
that burns inside of weakness,
only enlightened suffering
and an overwhelming vision
will be the ground for our joint being.
Nothing less would be a foundation,
would only shatter
when we assume our true weight
with time.

I sense your mind to be a trap
which catches me,
and my refusals to be caught
endanger what you call love.

But believe
that every time I step out
into a life without boundaries,
guided only by the compass
that is growing in me,
with your heart as its fixed point,
every time
you will grow richer
through all confusions
and denials.

All love is seeking,
and breaking through
to life beyond images.

I bloom
and become translucent.
My skin sings,
my senses open up,
I melt into the spring.
The risen one wins again
and death was only a servant.
Life finds a form
into which it can flow,
blossom-shaped, white and pink.

With these petals we can fly.
It is easy to lift off
because we are immortal.
We are still here
but stand in the light of transformation.
We cannot be held
and are without boundaries.

Life moves
in delicate ripples
from your center
and even in the faintest gentle stir
I sense the solid core
that energizes
what you touch.

Hope has a chance
where you appear.

The sun turns away
and allows the world to fall into its secret.
The trees are a row of witnesses
that pass on the secret.
As soon as the darkness settles on us
it begins to devour us,
but it is also nourishment.

It has settled on you and me also.
Your transitory cheek,
still bright and alive,
begins to fade.
I can sense the lightness of my blood
and the coolness of my hand.
And so it falls apart,
the small life.

But let us walk toward darkness,
experience the depth of the night,
in order to step into the different morning,
figures of light through and through.

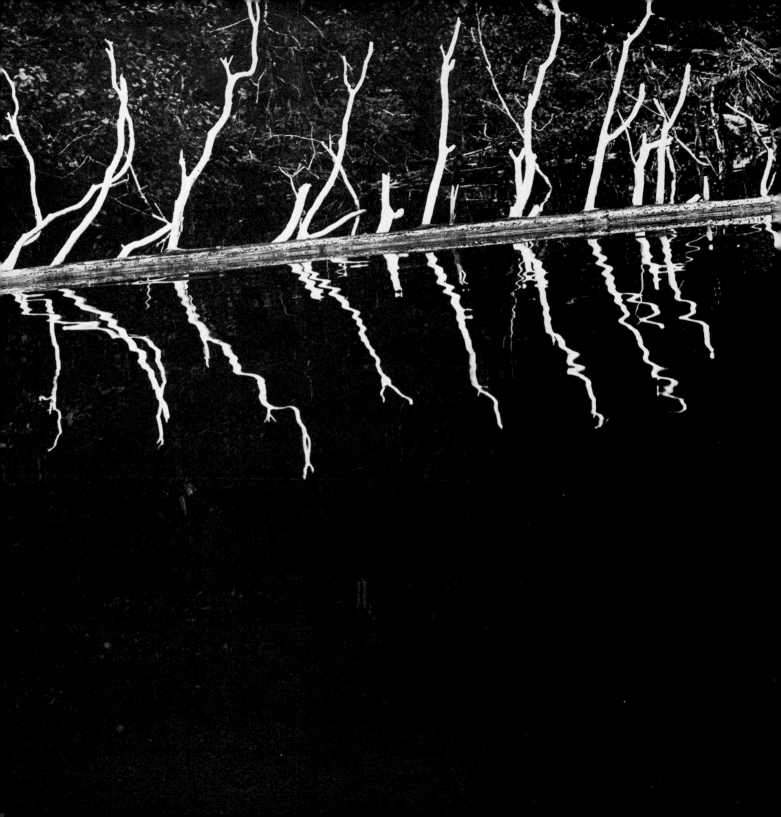

Death is in everything.

Brutally present with hammer and anvil
he is the smith of our end.
Or in fine filigree work
he hides between gold and silver,
and waits for the one
who has forgotten him.

He runs along
in the ticking of the clock.
He underlays the world
with gentle distortions,
so he will be mistaken
for someone else.
He steals colors
and paints everything in black and white.

And yet,
it is he who prepares us,
because he lets us feel our own skeletons,
so that we will become wise.

As gently
as these rocks rest against each other
I rest against your shoulder.

Bear me,
do not pull away
and turn to me.

And if we dare,
warmth will flow
even from stones,

the warmth which we so seek.

The intimate secret of your heart
gains in weight
as you allow time
to settle on your side.

I can sense it
in the weight of your eyes,
in the slowness of your speech,
in the value you give to detail.

I sense that you have embarked
on a journey to that inner world
to celebrate in silence
what will one day be.

Life surrounds you
like a colorful aura.
You surround your secret
like a wall, like a womb,

until it can be born.

These beeches
taking pains
to grow straight,
to reach the sun
in order to live.

We are walking under them,
subject to the same laws.
But for both of us there is enough sun.
I do not want to compete with you,
but rather lift you lovingly to the light,
scatter joy on your paths,
to interweave you, me and the sun
in a network of life.

And yet these fallen giants,
with their cold, smooth cut-wounds
point to the final law.
We can fall.
We will fall.
And only the light and fire
that we have taken in
will remain.

Our words
are once again
the signs of helplessness.
Arrows shot without conviction,
without soul or spirit.
They lack the energy
that seeks the heart.
They lack determination
that leads into pain.

Let's leave the alphabets of thought
and be in the becoming.
Let's watch the motion of the universe
as it expands from the light's core
and fills the void
with that one Word.

When you throw yourself into order
as if it were a last freedom
because you are afraid to live,
when you force yourself
to deny all becoming
and pretend to have arrived,
then I will not follow you.

That path you will have to walk alone.
I do not want to
come under the domination of rules again.
I no longer want to judge the world
according to right and wrong.
I want to experience and accept
the freedom
that I have been offered.
I want to learn to fly.

Do not go astray
in straightness.
Do not go under
in compulsions.
Do not choke
on correctness.

I am waiting for you.

Closed you stand before me.
No door is turned to me
and your eyes offer me no entry.

Yet I know
that a celebration is preparing itself in you
in silence and seclusion
and I will respect that and wait.

I don't know if you will invite me in later.
I will not wound you with expectations
nor confine you with suggestions.
I affirm your absence.

And if you open up to me again
I will take it as a gift,
and if you call me in,
I will come.

My pain
at your flight
when your own wind
propels you away:
when you are chaff
in your own eyes,
the kernel of truth
in mine.

Believe what you sense
when your mind embraces your soul
and your soul rests
in the bed of your body,
when warmth and light
affirm you
to the tips of your nerves.

Open your eyes
to the bud of love
wanting to bloom
between us.

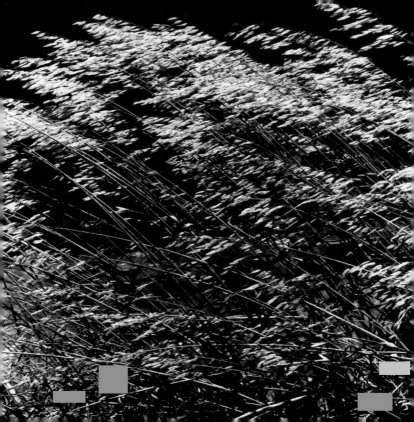

Again and again coldness attacks
to teach us dying.
It slows down the passage of life,
takes away the warmth
in which we can unfold.
With ice-fingers it points to limits.

You are becoming cold too,
bony in your love.
You are turning into the stranger
(in your rejection
more hostile than an enemy)
in whose presence
the thermometer drops.
My love fails with you,
but ultimately it just fails.

And yet,
because miracles only happen
if they are yearned for,
I now find reserves,
forgotten energies,
stored sunlight,
and in these ice crystals
I discover light,
so much light.

You might think
that I am breaking,
that I have fallen
and will not survive the storm,
but you are mistaken.
I am still growing.

I will not give up.
In desperation and hope
I will push down roots
into the hard ground.
You will see: I will live.

I gave up form and style long ago.
Survival in the gaping wound of life
is the goal which nourishes me.

I wrestle from life
the days needed for my fulfillment,
and when I finally do fall,
because in the end everything is a falling,
it will be upward
into the hands
of the waiting one.

My lostness
is my open eye.
My vision becomes keener.

The emptiness
gives the inner world a fullness.
Riches unfold.

I am preparing myself
for your presence.

I lose my direction
to search for a new one.
With you.

I empty myself
to receive you.
As you are.

In bleakness is our salvation.
And sometimes
the hand of love is a beckoning gray.

To me you are the survivor,
the one with stamina.
Catastrophes teach you to fight.
You don't accept the predictable as law.
You decide your life.
Under pressure, counter-pressure grows in you
and you become stronger.

You are tough
in the unmerciful weather.
In glaring sun
you demand more of yourself.
In the striking black and white world
you still discover the delicate grays.
For you there is no end
in time and space.

Take me with you
into courage.
Take me with you into the enlightenment
next to the abyss.
And in the middle of resistance
help me to learn the laughter of the child.

Up to our hips
we stand in grain.
It waves and grows
into our mouths.
We are fed.

And in the kernel of the grain
and in the heart of hearts
he is the bread.
Up to our hips
we stand in him.

He is
our life,
our dying,
life.

We differed little when we met.
We had our place and in it life,
from gray to black,
from good to worse.

And yet there was a hope
for open eyes,
for life and light,
a yearning for another land.

And when we fell,
we did not fall into each other's eyes
nor into love,
but into life.

And in our eyes
the searching God appeared,
no larger than our souls,
with features just like yours and mine.

Our wishes now are greater
than the world our arms embrace.
Our inner world is larger
than the outer.

The yearning finds its center
in our eyes,
and there he finds us
with such open hearts.

The order now is one of life
not death. And what we are,
we are like no one else.
Loved in a most abundant way.

I will not
explain myself to you
but test the tension
that our love can bear
without reverting back to deadly images,
to the despair of narrowness
or the hollowness of unbacked words.

I will remain where I am.
Please stay where you are,
centered in your being
and if our love is real
and more than an imitation
of that bright feeling
which nurtured us,
then it will create a giant arc
and bridge every gap.

No explanations will be needed.
Transformed, we will stand
in the flow of energy
and know everything.

At times the distance
to you
is unbridgeable.
I have to leave you
where you are.

But with time
you drift toward me,
even if you are rooted to the ground.
Or I give up my stability,
even though I am the shore,
and make my way to you.

We have to meet
to share our riches.

Postscript

While I was writing the texts in this book I had a list of my friends before me on my desk. I was addressing them, and I let them address me. Since every friend is different, each text turned out to have a different thought from the others. This strong emphasis on relationships is an expression of many experiences in my life in the last several years. In my first book of black and white photographs, *Searching for You*, almost all of the texts were directed toward God and were thus prayers. In this book I have put people in the center, in order to point out the presence of God, the body of Christ, as made present in men and women.

The concentration here on form and line, without the distraction of color, is a practice I find enriching. I hope the viewer of this book will find that also. Since the publication of *Searching for You*, my style has not changed essentially, although I have tried in this book to work more with light, airy photos, to put a greater emphasis on the white. When printing the pictures in the darkroom I still prefer the strong contrast. I therefore often use unusually hard photo paper. Most likely this preference is connected to my way of seeing the world. I do not wish to say much about the technical side of picture taking, because I believe now as before that good photography is the result more of how I see than of great technical knowledge.

I would like to thank my friends who helped me with the final selection of photos. A special thanks to Margie Carter and Coli Marinello for their inspiration at certain stages of the manuscript. It helped me greatly with some texts.

I hope that the readers and viewers of this book may come closer to finding the way to themselves and to God.

Notes on the Photos

7 Ocean, Point Lobos, California (1976).

9 Spiderweb with dew, Burnaby, British Columbia (1980). I was not primarily interested in photographing the web as a web, but in photographing the light in such a way that something quite ordinary becomes something precious.

10 Canoe with cliff face, Malibu, British Columbia (1979). I was intrigued by the overwhelming mass of rock and the small canoe, which seemed so helpless.

12 Chesterman Beach, Vancouver Island, British Columbia (1978). I have taken many pictures on this beach. The tree in the background stands on a rock which becomes an island at high tide. The pattern in the foreground changes with each tide. I have never again seen it as beautiful as it was on this day.

15 Landscape, California (1976). This landscape is very dry, and flooded by light. To indicate this, I printed the photo very light and made it into a graphic design.

16 Wood path, Bowron Lakes, British Columbia (1978).

19 Sheaves near Spences Bridge, British Columbia (1978).

20 Knotted root, Similkameen River, British Columbia (1976).

23 Rock pattern, Olympic Peninsula, Washington (1978).

25 Three sisters, Monument Valley, Arizona (1980).

26 Forest near Carmel, California (1979). I felt like I was looking into a fairytale forest.

28 Cariboo Falls, Bowron Lakes area, British Columbia.

31 Tree silhouette, near Bremen, Germany (1978). I underexposed this photo to emphasize the shape, the form of the tree. There is no symmetry here, no repetition. I never tire of looking at such trees. This is one of my favorite trees in the world.

33 Winter scene, Burnaby, British Columbia (1976).

34 Kelp, Carmel, California (1976).

37 Cypress on rock, near Carmel, California (1976). The almost desperate attempt of the tree to hang on, to survive, allowed me to see much more than a tree. It became a symbol for many situations in which I find myself, a symbol for life in general.

38 Foggy landscape near Carmel, California (1979). The different gray tones in the trunks and

needles gave the whole landscape something mysterious.

41   Tugboat in fog, Vancouver, British Columbia (1976).

43   Beach sand, Chesterman Beach, Vancouver Island, British Columbia (1978).

44   Dandelion, Burnaby, British Columbia (1976). I set up my camera in such a way that the sun was the same size as the dandelion. This makes the dandelion almost glow, as if lit from the inside. The fine lines and threads are made by a spider.

47   Boat, Steveston, British Columbia (1974).

49   Combers Beach, Vancouver Island, British Columbia (1980). At the shore of the ocean, I often have the feeling of being exposed, of being very vulnerable, especially if the beach is almost empty. When a person walked into the frame here I found a way of expressing this lostness.

50   Dune grasses, Oregon (1976).

53   Twisted cypress, Carmel, California (1976).

54   Old door hinge, Bodie, California (1976).

57   Blooming tree, Vancouver, British Columbia (1977).

58   Pond with small waves near Pitt Lake, British Columbia (1974).

61   Row of trees in black, northern Germany, (1977).

62   Skeleton tree in Bowron Lakes, British Columbia (1978). As I was canoeing, this tree and its reflection suddenly appeared. The small waves my canoe made distorted the reflection a little and offered a contrast to the image above the water.

65   Two rocks, Hornby Island, British Columbia (1977). The different surfaces and textures of these rocks, and their almost human forms, interested me.

66   Wall, Greece (1978).

69   Beech trees near Hannover, Germany (1977).

71   Combers Beach on Vancouver Island, British Columbia (1980).

72   Straight firs near Hannover, Germany (1977).

75   Whitewashed building, Greece (1978). In the three weeks I lived next to this house, it always remained something closed to me. I photographed it as though it had no door. The text picks up that idea again.

77   Grasses blowing in the wind, Greece (1978). I really wanted to photograph the wind.

78   Icicles, Burnaby, British Columbia (1981).

81   Stack off the Washington coast, Olympic Peninsula (1978). This is a rugged coast, with many stacks offshore. Many of these rocks sustain some sort of vegetation, even though there is very little soil there. I underexposed the picture (it was taken in streaming rain) to emphasize what seemed important to me.

82   Man alone in a boat, Elbe River, near Hamburg, Germany (1963). The state of many people: alone, adrift.

84   Door in Lindos on Rhodes, Greece (1978). I passed this door many times and was intrigued by its texture. To bring this out, I photographed it in the noon sun and printed the negative on very hard paper. This increased the black/white effect.

87   Field of grain near Wedel, Germany (1977). I crouched down and shot the photo up to give the feeling of being right in/under the field.

89   Canoes, Malibu, British Columbia (1979). The design of the floor boards and the lines fleeing toward the canoes caught my eye.

90   Olive tree, Rhodes, Greece (1978).

93   Lonely rock in the ocean, northern California (1976).

Ulrich Schaffer

with open eyes